To Kevin,
the werewolf who taught
our vampire girl not only
to dance, but to fly.

Text copyright © 2017 by Anne Marie Pace
Illustrations copyright © 2017 by LeUyen Pham
All rights reserved. Published by Disney • Hyperion,
an imprint of Disney Book Group. No part of this book
may be reproduced or transmitted in any form or by
any means, electronic or mechanical, including photocopying,
recording, or by any information storage and retrieval
system, without written permission from the publisher.
For information address Disney • Hyperion,
125 West End Avenue, New York, New York 10023.

First Edition, April 2017 • 10 9 8 7 6 5 4 3 2 1 • FAC-034274-17048
Printed in the United States of America
This book is set in 21-point Organically Medium/Fontspring
Illustrations were created in watercolor and pen-and-ink

Library of Congress Cataloging-in-Publication Data

Names: Pace, Anne Marie, author. | Pham, LeUyen, illustrator.
Title: Vampirina at the beach / written by Anne Marie Pace ; pictures by
    LeUyen Pham.
Description: First edition. | Los Angeles ; New York : Disney-HYPERION, 2017.
    | Summary: Vampirina, the little vampire ballet dancer, shows how to have
    fun and be safe at the beach.
Identifiers: LCCN 2016000636| ISBN 9781484773420 (hardcover picturebook) |
    ISBN 148477342X (hardcover picturebook)
Subjects: | CYAC: Vampires—Fiction. | Beaches—Fiction.
Classification: LCC PZ7.P113 Val 2017 | DDC [E]—dc23
LC record available at https://lccn.loc.gov/2016000636
Reinforced binding
Visit www.DisneyBooks.com

VAMPIRINA AT THE BEACH

WRITTEN BY
Anne Marie
Pace

PICTURES BY
LeUyen Pham

Disney • HYPERION
Los Angeles   New York

When the summer moon is full, a beach trip
is an epic way to spend the night.

Kick off the evening by helping to unpack the car.

You'll want a cooler full of yummy drinks and snacks to stave off hunger.

Don't forget the sunscreen!

Stake out your home base with a
colorful beach blanket and an umbrella.

Near a lifeguard stand is best.

There's a lot to do at the beach,
but you've got all night for fun!
Just pick anything and dive right in.

In the ocean,

always stay with a buddy

or two,

and only swim where the lifeguards can see you.

Playing in the waves can be a lot of fun.

Hop over low waves,

and dive through the high ones . . .

but never turn your back to the sea!

When the waves are breaking just right,
give surfing a whirl.

Practice your best ballet posture:

catch a wave,

demi-plié,

and ride,
ride,
RIDE!

You'll quickly learn
that wiping out

is part of the game.

As Madame always says,
"Chin up!"

It's hard to be the best
at something new.

Learning to snorkel might be
easier than learning to surf, but you
still have to concentrate.

Just remember to breathe through
your mouth and not your nose.

Once you're feeling comfortable in the
water, you'll discover . . .

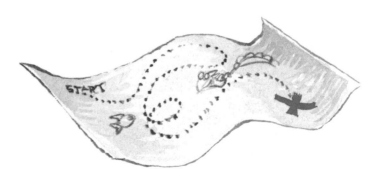

... all the hidden treasures of the ocean!

When you've had enough of the water,
ask your fellow beachgoers if you can join their
volleyball game.

Remember that volleyball is like dancing.

You must leap high,

stay light on your toes,

and always hit your mark.

After the game, try your hand
at a giant sand castle.

You'll need a big
shovel and bucket,

a pile of wet sand . . .

a bit of patience . . .

and a lot of ingenuity!

Just don't build too close to the water!

If the sand castle doesn't work out, don't worry. The night isn't over yet. . . .

Get stoked for a massive midnight dance contest!

As the night draws to an end,
sit around a roaring fire. Roast marshmallows
and hot dogs. Sing some old songs . . .

dancing with friends is fun
that never stops.

It doesn't matter if it's
Swan Lake on a stage

or the twist in the sand—

If the sand castle doesn't work out, don't
worry. The night isn't over yet. . . .

Whether or not you come out on top,

finishing with grace is what
makes you a real winner.

. . . and make plans for an encore!

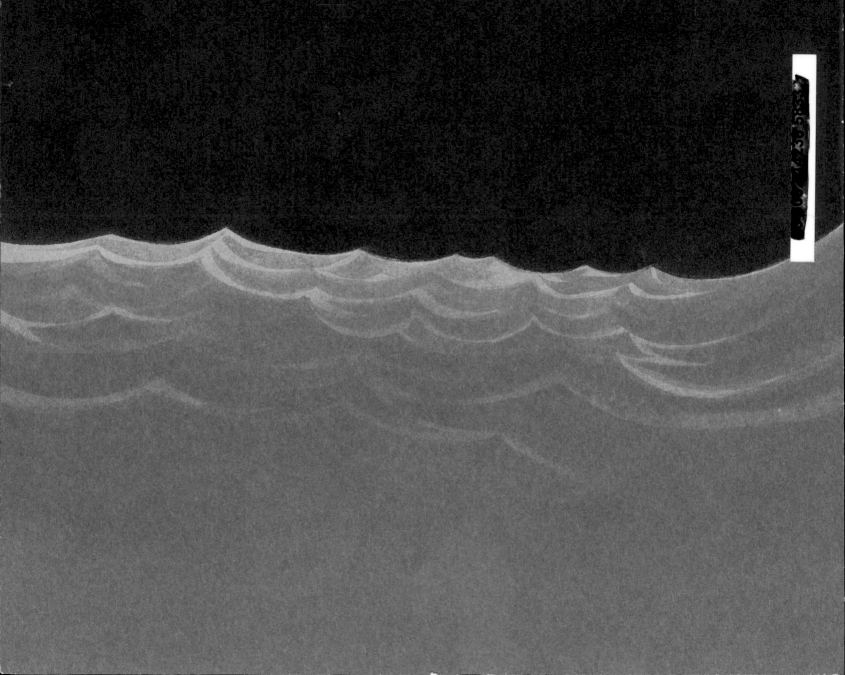

Tali's Jerusalem Scrapbook

by Sylvia Rouss
Illustrated by Nancy Oppenheimer

PITSPOPANY

NEW YORK ◇ JERUSALEM

Tali's Jerusalem Scrapbook
Published by Pitspopany Press
Text Copyright © 2003 by Sylvia Rouss
Illustrations Copyright © 2003 by Nancy Oppenheimer

Design: Benjie Herskowitz

Hard Cover ISBN: 1-930143-68-0
Soft Cover ISBN: 1-930143-69-9

Pitspopany Press titles may be purchased for fund raising programs
by schools and organizations by contacting:

Marketing Director, Pitspopany Press
40 East 78th Street, Suite 16D
New York, New York 10021
Tel: (800) 232-2931
Fax: (212) 472-6253
Email: pitspop@netvision.net.il
Website: www.pitspopany.com

Printed in Israel

Dedicated to the memory of

MARLA BENNETT

A beloved friend of my children, who cherished
the time she lived and learned in the city she
loved so much, Jerusalem.

ALSO BY SYLVIA ROUSS

The Littlest Frog

The Littlest Pair

2002 Storytelling World Award Winner

National Jewish Book Award Winner

The Littlest Candlesticks

10 Measures of beauty were
given to the world –
9 Measures can be found in
Jerusalem
1 Measure can be found in the
rest of the world

Talmud Kedushin 49b

Next week, my relatives from the United States are coming to visit my family in Jerusalem. They came last summer when my cousin Ben celebrated his Bar Mitzvah at the Western Wall. While they were here, we also celebrated my eighth birthday. My Aunt Sarah and Uncle David, and grandparents said they would return this summer.

I walked over to the shelf in my bedroom where I keep the gift my aunt and uncle gave me. It's a beautiful scrapbook. The leather cover is wrinkled and lined and reminds me of the soft creases on my grandparents' faces.

My *Sabbah* and *Saftah*, that's what I call my grandparents, always have wonderful stories to share. They tell me about their life in New York with its busy, noisy streets. I decided that my scrapbook would tell the story of my life in the city I love. I call it my Jerusalem Scrapbook.

When I was a little girl, I started collecting pictures of Jerusalem. Some are picture post-cards that my Ema and I purchased in the Old City, the part of Jerusalem that dates back thousands of years. I also have pictures that my Abba brought home from the Hebrew University where he teaches.

Last year, on my birthday, my grandparents gave me a camera. Now, I take my own pictures. I keep everything in my scrapbook.

I turned to the first page and gazed at a postcard of this beautiful city where I was born nine years ago, shortly after my parents moved to Israel from the United States. I thought about the many people who live here – Jews, Moslems, and Christians – and who, like me, love Jerusalem with its holy sites, parks, museums, and shops. All the buildings are made of Jerusalem stone. When the sun sets, the city shimmers as if made of gold.

Jerusalem means "City of Peace," but people have fought over this city for a long time.

I flipped to the page where I had pasted the very first photograph I took with my new camera. It was a picture of everyone gathered around my birthday cake – my grandparents, my Aunt Sarah and Uncle David, my cousin, Ben, Ema, Abba, and my little brother Micah. I smiled, remembering how happy we all were to be together.

Suddenly, I heard Ema call me, "Tali, it's time for breakfast."

I closed my scrapbook and joined Ema and Abba at the kitchen table. My little brother, Micah, was sitting in his chair. He began making faces at me.

"Sorry, Micah," I laughed, "I already have a picture of that one in my scrapbook!"

Just then, the phone rang. Ema answered it. "Hi Sarah," I heard her say, "We're all looking forward to your visit. Tali can't wait!"

Then I heard my Ema ask, "What do you mean you aren't coming? What about Mom and Dad?"

When my Ema hung up, she said, "Sarah's family cancelled their trip. She told me that David thinks Israel, and particularly Jerusalem, is unsafe right now."

"What about your folks?" my Abba asked.

"Without Sarah's family, they think the trip would be too difficult," my Ema replied.

"No!" I shouted. "That isn't fair!" I began to cry.

My Abba explained, "Tali, you know that many people are frightened by the violence that is happening here."

I nodded.

When I was born, we lived peacefully with most of our Arab neighbors. Now, there are some who want to hurt us. They don't want us to live here or anywhere else in Israel. They think that by hurting us, they can scare us away. They've attacked buses, markets, restaurants, and even the university where my Abba works. Many people have been injured or even killed.

Sometimes, I have nightmares. I dream that my family is on the bus or eating at a restaurant and someone comes to hurt us. I also worry about my Abba who drives near Arab neighborhoods every day on his way to work.

"Can't we visit them, Abba?" I suggested.

My Abba shook his head. "Others may be afraid to visit our home, but this is where we belong, especially now!"

My Ema gently added, "I know you're disappointed, Tali, but you'll still have a wonderful birthday. You can invite your friends, Dahlia and Leah, to join us."

I shrugged. "Ema, I just want to be alone for a while. May I go outside?"

My Ema nodded as I took my camera and headed outdoors.

I crossed the street to the park, sat on a bench, and wiped the tears from my eyes. When I looked up, I saw Mr. Feldman, who lives in my apartment building. Even though he is old like my grandfather, Mr. Feldman is my friend.

"What's wrong, Tali?" Mr. Feldman asked, as he sat down next to me.

I tearfully told Mr. Feldman, "My aunt's family and my grandparents decided not to come to Israel because it's too dangerous. I wish things could be like they were before all this fighting started."

"Yes," agreed Mr. Feldman, reaching into his pocket for a bag of bread. He handed me a slice and together we began feeding the birds. "We once worked side by side with the Arabs," he continued. "We traveled the same roads. We could visit the nearby Arab towns and feel safe. We helped some Arab villages build schools and medical clinics. Many Arabs became our friends. But things have changed because of those who want to hurt us."

I nodded sadly. "I know how my relatives feel. Sometimes I get scared too."

Mr. Feldman held out a handful of crumbs. I got up to take a picture as one bird actually began eating from his hand.

Mr. Feldman smiled and spoke softly, "Unfortunately, life is never perfect. It's okay to be afraid, but we can't give in to our fears. If we do, we truly stop living. Just because we find a big rock on the pathway of life, we can't simply stop in our tracks and wait for it to disappear. We have to figure out a way to go around that rock, or over it, so that we can enjoy all the remaining wonders along the pathway.

"Look at these birds," he said, pointing. "They never know from one day to the next what awaits them. Will they find food? Will another animal eat them? Even with this uncertainty, they still manage to entertain us with their singing."

"I wish my Aunt Sarah and Uncle David could figure out a way to go around the big rock," I said.

"If not this year, maybe next year," Mr. Feldman replied. "Some people take a little longer to continue on the path."

"Yes." I nodded hopefully.

Suddenly, I heard someone shout my name. I saw my friends, Dahlia and Leah, running towards us.

I smiled at Dahlia. There's a picture of her in my scrapbook when she was Queen Esther in our school Purim play. She has black wavy hair and her skin is the color of Ema's coffee after she adds cream to it. Dahlia's family is from Iran but, like me, she was born in Jerusalem.

"Hi," I said, looking at Leah's cheerful face. Her family moved to Jerusalem from Russia when she was a baby. Leah has red hair and freckles. When I take her photo, I never have to say, "Smile," because Leah always has a grin on her face.

"When are your relatives coming?" asked Dahlia.

"They're not coming," I sadly told her. "They're afraid."

"Maybe if only Jews lived in Jerusalem, they'd come." Leah remarked.

Mr. Feldman frowned, "I'm not sure you're right, Leah. Let's talk about it. But before we do, why don't you girls run to the store and pick up some ice cream for all of us." He handed me some money.

"Thanks, Mr. Feldman. What flavor do you want?" I asked.

"Surprise me!" he responded.

The three of us gave him a puzzled look as we ran off to the neighborhood store.

When we returned, I gave Mr. Feldman a nut covered ice cream bar. I'd selected chocolate for myself, Leah liked strawberry, and Dahlia was eating her favorite, a vanilla ice cream cone with sprinkles.

"What's your favorite flavor?" I asked Mr. Feldman.

"I like to try something different every time I eat ice cream. Can you imagine if there was only one kind to choose? It would be boring. Ice cream flavors are like the people who live in Jerusalem – all very different, but it's the differences that make this

an exciting place to live."

My friends and I looked at each other. None of us looked alike. We all came from other places. We lived in a city with many people from different lands and different religions. Mr. Feldman was right. Jerusalem wouldn't be the same if only Jews lived here. Dahlia held out her ice cream for me to taste. I gave Leah a lick of mine and asked Mr. Feldman to take a picture of us sharing our ice creams.

"I like tasting different flavors!" I exclaimed.

"Yum!" agreed Leah.

When Mr. Feldman left, I invited my friends to my house.

Micah was playing with his blocks while Ema was looking at her cookbook. "This recipe looks too difficult," she sighed.

"But Ema," I said, "You can't be afraid of things that you find on the pathway of life. Just because the recipe looks difficult, you can't let that stop you."

"Thanks for the encouragement, Chef Tali," she responded. "If you're willing to eat it, I guess I can prepare this liver stew."

I hurried to my bedroom with my friends, hoping Ema would make something else for dinner. I'll have to tell Mr. Feldman that some rocks just aren't worth climbing over.

"Can we see your Jerusalem Scrapbook?" asked Leah.

I took it off the shelf and showed them the pictures that Abba had brought home from the university. They were of Jerusalem a long time ago.

"Here's a picture of the Holy Temple. King Solomon built it over 2000 years ago. It was destroyed and today all that remains is the Kotel," I said pointing to a postcard of Jews praying at the Western Wall. "And here's a photo of my cousin, Ben, celebrating his Bar Mitzvah at the Wall last year."

"Since the fighting began, stones are sometimes thrown at the Jews praying by the Wall," Dahlia said sadly.

"Yes," agreed Leah. "My family used to walk through all parts of the Old City of Jerusalem. Now we just stay in the Jewish Quarter."

I turned the page. "That's a photo of my family eating at an outdoor café in the center of Jerusalem. We don't go there as much any more. Not since a restaurant in that area was attacked."

I thought about the liver stew and wished we could go to a restaurant this evening.

I giggled when I showed my friends a picture of my grandmother and me at the Jerusalem Zoo. We both had ice cream drips on our chins as we licked our cones.

"The next time my grandmother comes to visit I'm going to ask her to try a different flavor besides the vanilla she always eats," I told them.

"Here's a picture of Ema and me taking Micah on a bus ride. I enjoyed chatting with the other passengers as they fussed over my little brother. Now when I board a bus, I look at the other passengers and wonder if one of them wants to hurt me," I sighed.

"I feel the same way!" Leah exclaimed.

"I try to walk as much as possible," added Dahlia.

I turned the page to a postcard of the beautiful stained glass windows at Hadassah Hospital. Suddenly I thought about the ambulances I sometimes hear. I told my friends, "When I hear the sound of sirens, my heart beats so fast that I can't catch my breath. I'm scared there's been another attack and I pray that the ambulance is on its way to help someone sick instead. I know that isn't nice, but I can't help myself."

Leah wiped a tear from my eye while Dahlia hugged me. I thought, I'm lucky to have such good friends.

Finally, I came to the newspaper clippings folded between the pages of my scrapbook. "I'm not sure why I keep these," I confided. "Each time a 'bad thing'

happens in Jerusalem, I cut out the story. I haven't told Ema and Abba about them yet. I think it would upset them, but I believe these stories are important. I love Jerusalem and I would never want to live anywhere else, even with all the scary things happening here. I guess I keep the clippings because, in spite of the bad things, we still have many happy times. Someday, I'll show this scrapbook to my American relatives. Maybe then they'll understand that when you truly love something, you love it in good times and in bad."

As I gently closed my scrapbook, I heard Ema calling, "Tali, Abba's home from work."

Dahlia and Leah came with me to greet my Abba.

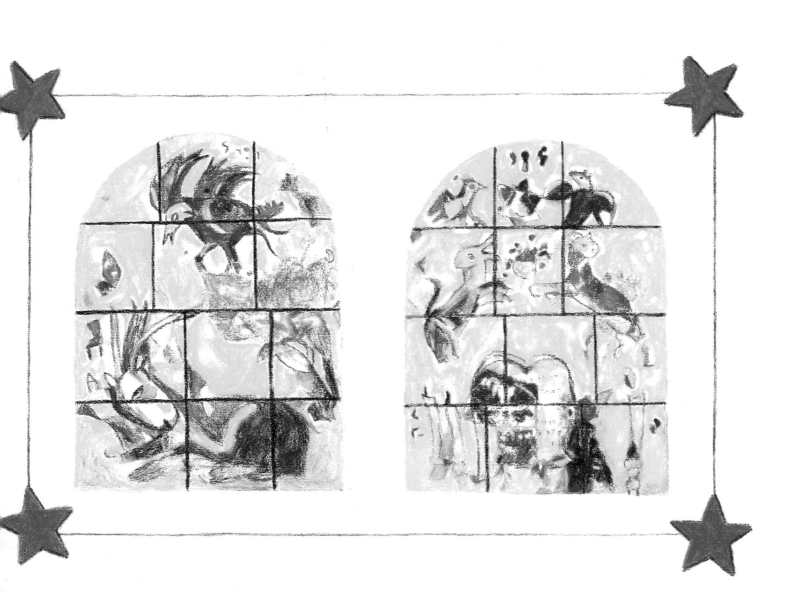

"Want some Bamba, girls?" Abba asked as he searched the kitchen cabinet for his favorite snack food.

"Micah finished the last of the Bamba today," Ema told my disappointed Abba.

"Abba," I suggested, "I can make popcorn. I know you like Bamba, but it's boring if you eat only one kind of snack food when you have so many choices – like nuts, or potato chips, or pretzels, or…"

"Okay, Tali, you've convinced me," Abba replied. "Go make popcorn."

Leah and Dahlia helped pop the corn. Afterward, I took a picture of all of us gathered around the table eating handfuls of popcorn.

"This is delicious!" Abba announced.

After my friends left, Ema and I set the table for dinner. I told her, "I'm not hungry. I think I ate too much popcorn."

"I'm sorry to hear that," replied Ema. "Here, Tali, just try a little," she insisted, dipping a spoon into the pot on the stove.

I closed my eyes and scrunched my face as Ema gave me a spoonful of liver stew. It tasted strangely like spaghetti with fresh vegetable sauce.

"This tastes good!" I exclaimed.

"I chose this recipe instead of the liver stew," she stated. "It was even more difficult to prepare." She filled a plate for me and set it on the table.

A week later, my birthday arrived. My parents surprised me by inviting Mr. Feldman to my party. Dahlia and Leah came with their parents.

Mr. Feldman suggested that we all talk about what we like best about our life in Jerusalem. Leah's Abba mentioned the Kotel, while Dahlia's Ema said the

synagogue. Abba said he enjoyed the museums with their wonderful exhibits, and Ema talked about the sidewalk cafés. Leah and Dahlia agreed that they liked the beautiful parks.

At last, it was my turn. I told everyone, "I love all the different people of Jerusalem." Mr. Feldman beamed at me when I said, "We're like the birds in the park. We never stop singing even though we don't know what might happen tomorrow or next week."

Abba took a picture of me blowing out the candles on my birthday cake. I closed my eyes and made a wish. For a special treat, Mr. Feldman had brought different kinds of ice cream. I smiled at Mr. Feldman as I handed each person a few spoons.

I reminded them that Jerusalem is made up of many people, all different, but special in their own way. I asked everyone to sample the ice cream flavors to see how truly delicious they all are. When I looked into the smiling faces of my family and friends, I thought about this city that has drawn people from different parts of the world together to make Jerusalem, the home we all love.

As I picked up my camera to take a picture of everyone, I wondered about my relatives. I felt sad that they had missed this happy occasion.

Softly, I repeated my birthday wish, "I hope next year you'll be in my Jerusalem Scrapbook."

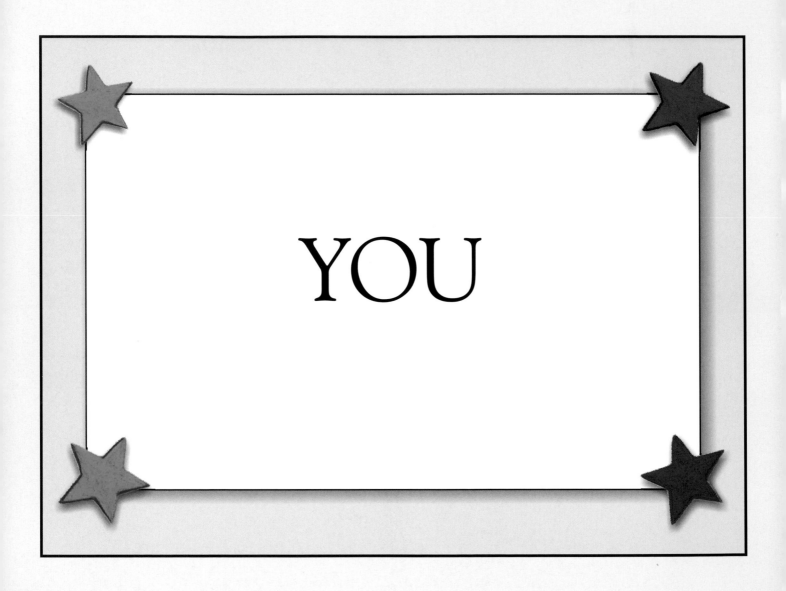

YOU